HAPPY FEET TWO

The Novel

D0190161

by Paul Livingston

PSS!
Price Stern Sloan
An Imprint of Penguin Group (USA) Inc.

PRICE STERN SLOAN
Published by the Penguin Group
Penguin Group (USA) Inc., 375 Hudson Street,
New York, New York 10014, USA
Penguin Group (Canada), 90 Eglinton Avenue East, Suite 700,
Toronto, Ontario M4P 2Y3, Canada
(a division of Pearson Penguin Canada Inc.)
Penguin Books Ltd., 80 Strand, London WC2R 0RL, England
Penguin Group Ireland, 25 St. Stephen's Green, Dublin 2, Ireland
(a division of Penguin Books Ltd.)
Penguin Group (Australia), 250 Camberwell Road,
Camberwell, Victoria 3124, Australia
(a division of Pearson Australia Group Pty. Ltd.)
Penguin Books India Pvt. Ltd., 11 Community Centre,
Panchsheel Park, New Delhi—110 017, India
Penguin Group (NZ), 67 Apollo Drive,
Rosedale, Auckland 0632, New Zealand
(a division of Pearson New Zealand Ltd.)
Penguin Books (South Africa) (Pty.) Ltd., 24 Sturdee Avenue,
Rosebank, Johannesburg 2196, South Africa

Penguin Books Ltd., Registered Offices: 80 Strand, London WC2R 0RL, England

HAPPY FEET TWO and all related characters and elements are trademarks of and
© 2011 Warner Bros. Entertainment, Inc. All rights reserved. Published by
Price Stern Sloan, a division of Penguin Young Readers Group,
345 Hudson Street, New York, New York 10014. *PSS!* is a registered trademark of
Penguin Group (USA) Inc. Printed in the U.S.A.

ISBN 978-0-8431-9819-5   10 9 8 7 6 5 4 3 2 1

Ramon has attitude, but never knows when to quit.

Chapter 1

On the southern side of Earth lies Antarctica, an ice- and snow-covered continent. One day, a massive iceberg snapped off the edge of the frozen landmass and plunged into the ocean. *Creeeech! Thwarrrrrk! Crrrrack! Phwhooompah!* But this iceberg was no ordinary floating mountain of ice. It was the Doomberg, and the Doomberg was on the move.

Meanwhile, a party was under way in Emperor Land—the home of a colony of Emperor penguins in Antarctica. Emperor penguins are known for braving dangerous conditions like blizzards and icy winds. But these Emperor penguins are also known for their happy, dancing feet and their singing.

Over a hundred gray-bellied, fluffy penguin chicks danced around Gloria, a beautiful, female Emperor penguin. She sang at the top of her lungs.

All the penguins in Emperor Land were dancing to the beat of thousands of happy feet. Among them stood Mumble, the famous tap dancing penguin who thrilled the crowd with his tippity-tip-tap feet. Even Noah the Elder, the leader of the Emperor penguins, stood high on his icy tower, moving his aging feet to the beat.

Below the tower, Ramon joined the celebration. Ramon was not a local; he was an Adelie penguin. You could tell by the patch of orange fur on his head and also by his height. Although he wasn't a kid, he was barely taller than the young Emperor penguins around him and only half the size of his best friend, Mumble.

Ramon was determined to impress every single female in Emperor Land. But even with his endearing Spanish twang, he had a hard time getting the attention of the ladies. The female penguins around him were busy

dancing to the beat of one of Emperor Land's finest elementary teachers, Miss Viola, as she yodeled loudly.

Miss Viola's daughter Bo (short for Boadicea) joined in, yodeling just like her mother.

"Yodelay, yodelayee," sang Bo, much to her mother's delight.

Nearby, big Seymour turned to his plump son Atticus and began his big daddy rap.

"Lift your head up, 'cause you're a star! Be strong, boy, you know who you are!"

Atticus rapped in response as he charged his way through a crowd of fluffy chicks.

The Emperor nation was alive with song and dance. Everyone was having a great time. Everyone except Erik . . . the tiniest, fluffiest penguin in all of Emperor Land.

Watching the celebration from behind a mound of ice, Erik peeped out at his friends, Atticus and Bo. They were shaking their little bellies while Erik's mother, Gloria, sang out to his father, Mumble. The beauty of Gloria's singing was matched only by the razzle-dazzle of Mumble's dancing feet. Erik's parents were

the centers of attention, the golden stars of Emperor Land.

Suddenly, the party swung in Erik's direction. Erik huddled into the ice, trying to make himself even smaller. But there was nowhere to hide. Before he knew it, a wave of young, dancing penguins swept him into the center of the icy dance floor.

All eyes were on Erik, but he didn't budge. He didn't dance. He just stood still. If penguins could blush, Erik would have turned bright red.

When Mumble and Gloria spotted their little boy frozen in fear, they stopped dancing.

"Aw, my little munchkin," Gloria said. "I'll go talk to him."

"Let me try," Mumble offered, walking toward Erik.

"Hey, little guy. You okay? You're not joining in?" asked Mumble.

Erik stared at the ice and shook his head.

"Can you say why?" coaxed Mumble.

"Why?" said Erik.

"No, no," Mumble corrected. "What I mean is . . ."

"Uncle Mumble?" Boadicea interrupted. "I think he's asking why dance?"

"Like, he needs a solid reason," Atticus put in. "Don't ya, Erik?"

Erik nodded.

"But there are plenty of reasons to dance!" Mumble told him.

"What's mine, Pa?" Erik asked.

"Well, the only way to know is to try it," offered Mumble, tapping out a move with his feet. "C'mon, son. It's just one big ol' foot after the other. All you've got to do is feel the beat! Hop onto my feet!"

Mumble scooped Erik up onto his dancing feet. All the other young penguins joined in.

"Now you try," encouraged Mumble, putting Erik back on the ice.

Erik just stood there.

"If you can't say it, you can sing it, and if you can't sing it, you can dance it!" urged Mumble.

Erik took a deep breath. To Mumble's delight, he took a few steps.

But Erik's moves were really goofy! So goofy, in fact, that Mumble couldn't help but let out a small chuckle. Before long, the whole crowd— toddlers and adult penguins—started to giggle.

Erik was painfully aware that the laughter

was directed at him. He soon lost his balance, his feet and flippers flailing as he frantically attempted to remain upright.

Thwack! Erik fell flat on his beak. He skidded on the ice, slid through a mushy puddle, and went down a steep incline. *Swoosh!* He flipped high into the air, flapping his fins in a desperate attempt to fly. But, as everyone knows, penguins can't fly.

Splat! Erik landed headfirst in a hole full of icy water, his little legs wiggling wildly in the air. Penguins from the crowd laughed even more.

Gloria rushed to her son's aid. As Erik lay on his back, a tiny fountain of pee squirted into the air. Again, more laughter could be heard. Mumble was mortified.

Bo and Atticus quickly came to Erik's defense.

"It's not funny," Bo told the crowd.

"Can you wizz on cue and finish with a headstand? I don't think so," Atticus added.

Gloria helped her son onto his feet.

"Are you okay? Are you hurt?" she asked, giving him a hug.

Erik stepped back.

"Oh gosh, Erik, that was, kind of, wow . . . ,"

Mumble said, searching for a compliment.

Erik looked up at his father, his face full of hurt. He turned, ran toward a small ice crevice, and jumped in. The other little penguins gathered around, trying to take a peek at Erik in his hidey-hole.

"Erik, I'm really sorry. We all get off on the wrong foot sometimes," Mumble said, trying to coax his son out of the crevice.

But Erik was not about to be humiliated again. He stayed put.

"C'mon, champ," Mumble continued. "It wasn't that bad. When I was your age, I got laughed at a lot. They thought I was weird, too . . . I mean, different, you know . . . in a cool way, I was totally uncool. Really uncool."

Mumble was trying to help. He really was. But the only thing that Mumble was doing was making things worse!

Chapter 2

While Mumble was busy with his son, Ramon was busy with the female penguins.

"I would never have an egg with him," said one female in disgust.

"Give me one good reason!" demanded Ramon.

"You're too short . . . and gross!" she hissed. But Ramon never knew when to quit.

"Not if you close your eyes," he said, puckering his beak. Ramon cracked one eye open and saw the female walking off with a tall, handsome Emperor penguin.

"Is that guy bothering you?" the Emperor penguin said, nodding at Ramon.

"No, he's nobody," she replied.

Ramon's pucker turned to a quiver. He

shuffled off slowly with a heavy, broken heart. He walked straight past Mumble and Gloria and hopped into the crevice with Erik.

"So you were mocked and misunderstood, too?" Ramon said.

Erik nodded.

"They don't deserve us," Ramon said.

"Ramon!" cried Mumble.

"What?" said the defeated Ramon.

"This is between Erik and me!" hinted Mumble.

Ramon popped his head out of the icy hole.

"Don't worry. I can fix it," he confided. "What's a best friend for if he can't bring a daddy and his boy together?"

Mumble was far from convinced. "Thanks, but not now . . ."

Ramon wasn't listening. He turned to Erik.

"You know, little fluffito? The truth is, for wild maverick outcasts like us who can't be tamed . . . this place sucks!"

"Ramon, you're being ridiculous!" called Mumble from above.

"Not anymore!" Ramon shot back. "I'm going home to Adelie Land!"

He lifted himself out of the crevice and started walking away. Erik raised his head out of the hole and watched as Ramon headed off.

"Adelie Land! Adelie Land! Be who you want to be! A haven for heroes, just like you and me. Thrills and adventure, that's our guarantee!" Ramon sang as he walked.

Erik liked the sound of that. His face lit up.

Mumble leaned forward into the crevice.

"Erik? Are you okay?"

Erik didn't respond.

"Honey, I think he needs to be alone right now," said Gloria.

"We can't leave him all by himself!" said Mumble.

"We've got his back, sir!" cried little Bo as she backflipped into the hole. Hot on her heels was Atticus. He tried the same trick, but got stuck for a second before slipping in.

"So much for my daddy skills," moaned Mumble.

Mumble walked away and saw Ramon standing at the entrance of Emperor Land.

Ramon stood as tall as an Adelie penguin could and shouted, "Adios, all you Emperor

ladies! This is one fabulous penguin you'll never laugh at again!" Then Ramon turned and marched toward a white, icy horizon stretching out to the open sea.

♫

Somewhere in the great ocean, the massive Doomberg was still in motion. Suddenly, it lurched and tilted, breaking into pieces and sending enormous chunks of ice into the water. *Kak-ak-ak-fushooshh!* A huge, rolling wave formed, moving closer and closer to . . . who knows where?

♫

Some time later, Mumble, Gloria, Seymour, and Miss Viola returned to the crevice to check on their children. Seymour carried a large fish in his beak, a treat for his boy.

"Hey, Atticus!" Seymour called. "Snack time!"

There was no sound from the crevice. Miss Viola thought the kids must have fallen asleep. But when Mumble bent over and peeked in, there was no sign of Atticus, Bo, or Erik. The

little penguins were gone!

Frantically, the adult penguins began to search for their children. First they looked through ice caves in the area and then on higher ground, across huge mounds of ice.

Mumble felt guilty about Erik's disappearance.

"Mumble, c'mon. He's an independent little guy, trying to find his own feet. You were exactly the same," Gloria told him.

Mumble listened, but his mind was elsewhere. He stood staring at the entrance of Emperor Land, wondering if the kids could have run off. He asked Gloria, but she thought that was ridiculous. The little penguins . . . by themselves? Never!

"Maybe they followed Ramon," said Mumble.

"Mumble, relax," said Gloria. "We will find them here, and when we do, you'll find a way to put things right. You're a good dad."

Mumble hoped Gloria was right, but he had doubts.

"I really ought to check it out," he said. "I'll be back as soon as I can." And with that, he headed out of Emperor Land.

Chapter 3

Not far away, a huge wave caused by the Doomberg rolled on and on across the ocean. Deep below, a swarm of tiny, pink, shrimplike creatures called krill was tossed by the powerful wave. In the center of the huge swarm, two translucent krill named Bill and Will paddled frantically, just to keep steady.

"Whoa! That was a big 'un!" yelped Bill.

"I hate it when that happens," squeaked Will.

"Hey, Will? Is that you?"

"Of course it's me, can't you tell?"

"Not if we all look the same."

"I don't look the same," Will protested.

"Will, we are krill. We are meant to look the same."

"Not me, Bill. There is only one of me in

the whole world. I'm one in a krillion," Will insisted. He pivoted around and swam against the tide of the swarm.

"Will, where are you going?"

"I'm leaving. I want to be free, Bill."

"There is no such thing as free, Will!" said Bill in a panic. "Come back. Less thinking, more swarming."

"I'm sick of swarming, Bill. We've been swarming all our lives."

Bill struggled to swim against the swarm and keep up with Will.

"Sometimes, Will, it's like you've got a mind of your own."

Will zipped in and out of the oncoming krill, enjoying the thrill.

"Tell me, Bill, what do you think lies beyond the swarm?"

"More swarm, I would imagine."

"And then what?"

"Some more swarm?"

"And then?" Will persisted.

"Will! There is nothing but swarm," said Bill. "We are swarm without end."

"Everything's got an end, Bill. It stands to

reason, if I swim against the swarm, I must eventually reach the end of the world."

As the krill were swimming, Ramon stood on an icy ledge and peered into the ocean. He was trying to talk himself into diving in to find some food—fish, or maybe a krill or two.

Ramon counted to three and then hurled himself toward the edge. But he dug in his heels at the last second. He was too scared. He tried to reason with himself.

"I can do this."

"No, you can't."

"Yes, I can do this."

"No, you can't."

"Who's talking to me?"

"You."

"Who are you?"

"Me."

"Who said that?"

"I did."

As Ramon bickered with himself, a huge wave broke over the ice and washed him farther away from the shoreline. When he lifted

his head, he was surprised to see three small penguins: Atticus, Bo, and Erik, all sliding on their bellies toward him.

"We're coming to Adelie Land!" chirped Bo with glee.

"Oh, no, you aren't," warned Ramon. "You're out here without your parents. I'll be arrested for chick-napping! Now go. Shoo! Shoo!"

Bo explained they were fugitives on the run.

"No happy feets," chimed in Erik.

"Rebels seeking thrills and adventure," added Bo.

"And tasty snacks!" said Atticus.

The mention of food got Ramon's interest. He liked the idea of someone else fishing for him.

"Okay, I want a big fish, three little ones, and some of those teeny-weeny krill. Off you go!" said Ramon, pointing a flipper toward the ocean.

"But we can't swim," said Bo. "We're too fluffy!"

"Fluffy don't float," said Erik.

The three kids looked at Ramon. After all,

Ramon was the adult, so he should be the one to do the fishing!

"But it's too far down! I'm a leapophobic," said Ramon, shivering in fear.

Atticus was starving. So starving, in fact, that he started gnawing on his own flipper!

"Okay, okay." Ramon stepped in before Atticus could do any damage. "Here's what we do. We count to three. Push me on two, but don't tell me, okay?"

Atticus and Bo immediately started to count. "One! Two!" Then they pushed Ramon into the water. He disappeared momentarily but soon resurfaced, muttering to himself, "Baby penguins. Cute . . . but ruthless."

As Ramon was bobbing on the surface, Bill and Will were talking deep down below.

"What are we looking for, exactly?" asked Bill.

"That's the beauty of it, my friend," said Will. "I don't know!"

At that moment, Will saw a break in the swarm—his first glimpse of open water. He

sped toward it. Ever cautious, Bill frantically tried to dissuade him.

"Will, please! Come back! I fear the worst!"

"I fear the worst, too, Bill, because fearing the best is a complete waste of time."

As they were leaving the safety of the swarm, they saw a scary-looking shadow.

"A black hole!" cried Bill, recalling the ancient krill legends of black holes coming out of nowhere, swallowing everything in their paths.

"Relax, they're just stories. Scary talk," said Will, fascinated by the growing black shadow. "Mind you, for something that doesn't exist, it's quite impressive."

"Swim! Swim for your life!" Bill squealed, grabbing Will and pulling him back. At that moment, Bill and Will realized that the black hole was actually the mouth of an enormous Humpback whale. The gigantic creature plunged into the swarm, swallowing masses of krill. Then, smaller black holes appeared as schools of hungry fish joined in the feeding frenzy.

Just before a speeding fish was about to swallow Bill and Will, Ramon appeared out of

nowhere and came to a sudden halt. He was staring at twin black holes heading straight for him.

But these black holes were really two very scary Leopard seals!

"Penguin munchers!" screamed Ramon, swimming for his life.

Spotting Ramon, the two Leopard seals chased him.

Back on the ice, Atticus, Bo, and Erik watched as Ramon shot out of the water. When he landed, he shook with terror.

"Take me home!" he begged the baby penguins.

Under the water, Will and Bill were separated from the swarm. Having just seen the Humpback whale and schools of fish eat countless krill, they now understood their place in the world.

"So this is all we are?" said Will. "Lunch?"

A tear filled Bill's eye.

"Good-bye, krill world," he said.

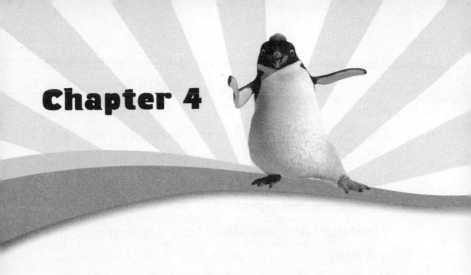

Chapter 4

Meanwhile, Mumble had left Emperor Land to search for Erik, Atticus, and Bo. Soon he spotted a fresh set of tracks. *Ramon!* thought Mumble. He flopped on his belly and slid down a long slope toward Adelie Land.

Not too far away, Ramon and the kids looked out across Adelie Land. The four penguins had made their way to Ramon's homeland. The area was surrounded by ice cliffs on one side and the ocean on the other.

Below, Erik, Atticus, and Bo saw thousands of penguins just like Ramon—no taller, but no shorter, either. And in among these Adelie

penguins were many other types of penguins, all assembled around a large mound covered in green moss and grass. The kids had never seen anything like it before.

Ramon was home! He raced down the slope straight toward Lombardo, Rinaldo, Raul, and Nestor—his closest friends.

"Ramon?! Ramon!" they exclaimed.

Ramon introduced the kids to his Amigos.

"So tell me, where are all the Ramon-starved chicas?" Ramon asked.

"Man, you've been away too long. There's a lot more competition now," said Lombardo.

Suddenly, a roar rang out from the crowd as Lovelace, a strange-looking penguin, stepped onto the grassy mound. Lovelace was a squat Rockhopper penguin with a brightly colored knitted vest that had green, pink, and blue stripes around it and a yellow heart in the middle. There was a story behind this vest. And Lovelace loved to tell it.

"Lovelace! Lovelace!" chanted the crowd.

Ramon was upset that all the penguins around him only paid attention to Lovelace and not to him. "Worst case of feather rot I've

ever seen," he said, glaring at the vest.

"Brothers and sisters," Lovelace called out, waving his flippers around wildly. "We are many kinds gathered here from far and near. Because it's a new day in a new age! In an all-new Adelie Land! For this is the time of Sven!"

At the sound of *Sven*, the crowd cheered.

"Sven! The Mighty Sven!" they chanted.

Ramon was confused. Who was Sven?

"I want you all to make your flippers quiver and your beaks shriek. It's SvenTime!" cried Lovelace.

Lovelace pointed to the top of an iceberg, and the crowd burst into wild applause. There, backlit by the sun, Sven stood majestically.

Sven was a barrel-chested penguin with an oversized, battle-scarred, red beak and golden feathers swept back across his head. He held up a flipper, instantly hushing the adoring crowd. Then, he thrust his beak in the air and leaped off, dropping like a stone down the face of the iceberg.

Erik, Atticus, and Bo let out a gasp. Surely no penguin could survive a fall from that height! But then, the most amazing thing happened.

Just before Sven hit the water . . . *whoosh!* With one sweep of his flippers, he soared high into the air, at first higher than the peak of the iceberg, and then higher still.

Erik rushed forward, wide-eyed. A penguin that could fly!

Female penguins trampled over Ramon as they surged toward Sven. The flying penguin swooped over them, dazzling the crowd with a series of loops, rolls, spins, and spirals.

Then Sven's feet extended beneath him and he set himself down on the mound next to Lovelace.

"Your story. Tell it, brother," Lovelace urged.

"Oh, but friends," said Sven. "It such a long story," he said with his unusual accent and choice of words.

"Tell the short one," shouted Ramon.

Sven began his story with great seriousness.

"It all begin with the loss . . ."

"Hey, Goldilocks!" Ramon interrupted. "That beak looks way too big on you!"

"Keep it down, clown," Lovelace warned Ramon.

Sven composed himself and started over.

"It begin . . ."

"The end!" barked Ramon, quite pleased with himself. But he got no laughs from the audience.

"Security!" Lovelace called. Almost instantly, Ramon was held back by a troop of security Chinstrap penguins.

Erik was awestruck by Sven and saw his chance to get closer. He darted past the security penguins and toward the stage, closely followed by Atticus and Bo.

Lovelace turned to Sven. "I'm still here for you, brother. I will help tell your story."

"Okay, I give it another try," Sven agreed. "It begin with the loss of my home." But then he stopped.

"No, no, the moment is gone. Forget about . . . maybe tomorrow," he said.

The crowd urged Sven to continue. But Sven would not budge.

"No, I'm sorry! I'm not feeling it. Show's over!" he said.

As Sven turned to leave, he felt a tug on his tail feathers.

"Please, sir? My friend has a question," said Bo.

Sven turned to see three baby penguins staring up at him in wonderment. The littlest one asked shyly, "Does your story have flying in it?"

"Where you from, little squirt?" said Sven.

"We from da Emperor-hood," Atticus butted in.

"What *your* name is?" said Sven.

"Erik."

Erik's hopeful eyes gave Sven a change of heart about telling his story. He invited Erik to join him onstage. Erik took a few steps onto the grass. It tickled his feet.

"Ya, okey-doke. Hey, everybuddy," said Sven, addressing the crowd. "I now dedicate my much-applauded, heartwarming saga to my brave friend . . . III-RIK!"

The entire crowd began to chant Erik's name with Sven's strange accent. "III-RIK! III-RIK!"

For the first time in his short life, Erik's chest swelled with pride.

High on a ridge overlooking Adelie Land stood Mumble, astonished to hear a crowd of penguins below chanting his son's name.

Center stage, Lovelace began to tell Sven's story, with Sven filling in some of the details.

27

Chapter 5

The Story of Sven—as told (mainly) by Lovelace

Once upon a time, on an arctic glacier, an enormous volcano erupted and spewed huge plumes of ash into the air.

Sven was the last of a noble penguin race whose world collapsed without warning.

"My homeland was destroyed, and I alone escaped the disaster," Sven explained.

As Sven fled, a cloud of ash peppered with lightning flashes blocked out the sun.

"My power to fly was my saving grace," added Sven.

Through his incredible feats of flying, Sven traveled over a vast ocean until he managed to land on the tip of an iceberg. He was in bad shape and so exhausted he could fly no farther.

But as the iceberg began to drift south and melt, it got smaller and smaller.

Soon all that was left of the iceberg was a tiny raft of ice. And just before it all melted away, Sven bumped up against a wall of red metal. It was the hull of a scientific research ship.

"The humans took me in and fixing up my injuries. Soon, I'm resting on a pillow in a woven basket, plaster casting covering me from feet to beak," Sven said.

As the ship headed south, Sven waddled along the deck of the ship, still wearing the brace to keep his body upright. Suddenly, he noticed something on the horizon. A damaged oil tanker was leaking oil into the ocean, and a penguin was stuck in it, gasping for air! Sven made a loud, honking sound, which drew the attention of the ship's crew. They rescued the penguin by scooping him into a net.

"That penguin was Lovelace!" declared Sven.

I lay in the ship's laboratory while scientists rubbed me down to remove the oil covering my feathers. Sven watched as they blow-dried me and fitted me with a colorful knitted vest to keep me warm.

One day, Sven and I were strolling along the ship's deck as one of the scientists was playing a guitar. Around him, other crew members without instruments pretended to play along with him. I loved the music and began grooving to the beat, delighting the scientists. Before long, I was playing my own imaginary guitar. The humans called it air guitar. But just when I thought we had found a new home on this ship with our new "family," Sven saw something that made him realize our destiny lay elsewhere. With his beak, he suddenly tore off his remaining bandages.

"I knew it was time to leave . . . QUICKLY!" Sven announced.

Sven leaped from the side of the ship and flew away. I realized then that he could fly!

I jumped into the sea to follow him. Eventually, we arrived on the shore of Adelie Land. Curious penguins edged closer, staring at the flying penguin and something sprouting between Sven's toes: a blade of green grass.

"Soon after my landing, patches of green grass sprouting up all over Adelie Land, courtesy of me!" Sven declared.

Chapter 6

As soon as Sven's story was finished, the crowd started chanting his name again.

"The Mighty Sven! The Mighty Sven!" they shouted.

Sven held up a flipper. "From that day I took a vow: I, Sven, promise to use my powers for goody. When I fly, my flippers will warm the air and melt the ices!"

"No more frozen butts!" yelled Lovelace.

Sven took to the air and glided gracefully over the crowd and then high into the sky.

"And I dedicate full time to the creation of a New Adelie Land!" cried Sven.

At that instant, Adelie Land began to rumble and shake. Mumble, who had been making his way through the crowds of adoring penguins, looked around nervously. What was that?

The penguins did not know it, but the rumble was caused by the Doomberg. It was on the move, bumping along the ocean floor, destroying everything in its path!

As the rumbling stopped, the crowd erupted into cheers and applause. They thought the tremor was caused by the powers of Sven!

Sven, at first uneasy, accepted the crowd's admiration for the disturbance. He put on his most heroic face and flew low overhead, delighting the female penguins below.

"Sven! Marry me!" one of them cried out.

"Ah, my beauty, but if I should love only you, who will love them?" Sven said, gesturing to all of his devoted followers.

This prompted Ramon to speak up defiantly. "Okay, already, but who will love Ramon?"

Instantly recognizing that voice, Mumble pushed his way through the crowd toward Ramon. Sven landed on top of a penguin's head and addressed Ramon.

"Ah, bitter, twisted, lonely guy. You must learn to think like Sven."

Sven touched both flippers to his temples.

"If you want it, you must will it!" Sven

instructed. "If you will it, it will be yours!"

"SvenThink! SvenThink!" chanted the crowd.

Ramon was not convinced by this "SvenThink."

"I'll prove it doesn't work," he said, clamping his flippers to his temples.

"Now empty your mind," said Sven.

"Done," said Ramon. "Too easy."

"Now picture your goal and will it!"

Ramon closed his eyes.

"Harder! Now with added bonus will!" Sven urged.

Ramon did his best to will it.

"Now open your eyes!" commanded Sven.

When Ramon opened his eyes, the first thing he saw was Mumble rushing toward him.

"Ramon! Where are the kids?" yelled Mumble.

Hearing Mumble's voice, the kids made themselves invisible by hiding behind Ramon.

Sven was not happy with this interruption of his SvenThinking session. With a wave of his flipper, a group of security Chinstrap penguins pounced on Mumble and wrestled

him to the ground.

"Okay, will it again. Will it!" Sven urged.

Ramon closed his eyes and willed his favorite wish. This time, when he opened his eyes, standing before him was Carmen, the prettiest penguin Ramon had ever seen.

"Thank you, SvenThink," Ramon muttered as he swaggered toward her. "You. Me. Egg. Now!"

Carmen sized him up.

"You. With Carmen? Fat chance!" she said coldly. Ramon took encouragement from her words. "I have a chance, and it's fat!"

Carmen turned her back and walked away.

"There goes the love of my life," said Ramon, following her. "Wait, Carmen. Wait!" Ramon's departure left Erik, Atticus, and Bo in full view.

Mumble broke free from the Chinstraps and raced toward them.

"ERIK! KIDS!" yelled Mumble, stopping the trio in their tracks.

"We're leaving. Right now. Let's go home," Mumble insisted.

"But this place is so much fun!" Bo objected.

"Come on, all of you!" said Mumble.

Erik refused to move.

"Erik, it's a long way home. Let's go!" ordered Mumble.

Erik still wouldn't budge.

"I'm not going back to Emperor Land," he said, turning his back on his father. "I'm staying here."

Mumble was getting more and more upset. "What about the folks back home and how worried your mother must be?"

Sven saw what was happening. He gave Mumble a nod and walked up to Erik.

"It best to do what your father says," Sven said.

"But I don't belong there," Erik replied.

Sven leaned in and whispered to Erik.

"Fluffy one, let me tell you little secret. Sometimes when you a little different, the world laugh at you."

Erik knew this only too well.

"We have a saying in Svenland. Believe in yourself, brave Iii-rik, because Sven believe in you."

Erik looked to his father, then back to Sven.

"Mighty Sven?" asked Erik. "Will I ever fly?"

"If you will it, it will be yours," Sven replied.

Erik gave Sven a big hug before heading off to join his father.

Mumble, Erik, Atticus, and Bo headed home to Emperor Land.

"You know, son, when things go wrong, running away is not the answer. You have to find a way to handle it. We're all different; it's part of the job of life to find out who you are and what you got. Right?"

Erik nodded.

"It may not be dancing or flying, but when you find it, it'll be all yours! Your thing! You know what I'm saying?"

"Ya, okey-doke." Erik imitated Sven's voice before running ahead to catch up with Atticus and Bo. Mumble realized Erik was not really listening.

Just then, the ice beneath their feet rumbled and shuddered. Erik fell on his back, and Atticus landed on his belly. Mumble and Bo were barely able to keep their balance.

On a beach nearby, a tribe of enormous

Elephant seals stopped their jostling as the ice beneath them shook, too. Out in the ocean, Leopard seals sleeping on ice floes were woken up.

Back in Emperor Land, the sound of the moving ice was deafening. Gloria led a group of penguin chicks away from the noise to safe ground. From his icy tower, Noah watched in horror as an enormous mountain of ice plowed its way toward Emperor Land. The Doomberg had arrived!

Still some distance from home, Atticus, Bo, and Erik were concerned.

"Uncle Mumble?" asked Atticus. "Are we okay?"

Mumble didn't know what kind of damage the shaking had caused, but he didn't want to worry the kids.

"Sounded awfully close to Emperor Land," said Bo.

Mumble frowned. "Come on, guys. Let's pick up the pace."

He wondered if they would be able to get back to Emperor Land safely.

Chapter 7

Meanwhile, under the ice, the two little krill rode out a powerful wave.

"What was that?" asked Bill.

"That is the wave of change," Will replied. "Adapt or die!"

"Adapt?" said Bill. "There's no telling what we might become."

"Fine," said Will. "Be a plankton muncher all your life."

"But that is what we are, Bill. We're herbivores. We eat veggies."

"Right, so everyone else can eat us," snapped Will. "Well, I for one am not prepared to be on the menu any longer."

Will turned and swam up toward the surface.

"Where are you going?" asked Bill.

"I'm moving up the food chain."

"The food chain?"

"That's right, Bill. I'm gonna chew on something that has a face!"

Mumble stood at the edge of a deep, wide crack in the ice. This crevasse stretched in either direction as far as the eye could see.

"I don't remember this being here," said Mumble. "We'll just have to go around."

"But Emperor Land is straight ahead," Bo insisted and pointed her flipper at a bridge of ice over the chasm. Mumble didn't trust it.

"No. This way is safer," he said, heading off.

"But shortcuts are shorter," Bo argued.

Mumble turned around to make sure the kids were following him. But they weren't there—they had already begun crossing the dangerous ice bridge.

"Kids! Stop! It's not safe!" yelled Mumble.

Bo and Atticus stopped midway across the bridge, but Erik kept going. Mumble hurried over to join the kids and shuffled across the narrow path, hoping his weight wouldn't bring

down the bridge. When he caught up to Bo and Atticus, and finally to Erik, he said, "Okay, we're going to have to keep going, but take it nice and slow. And don't look down."

Of course, Atticus immediately looked down and was terrified.

Then Mumble looked across the bridge and saw another scary sight—a humongous Elephant seal blocking their path!

"Where ya headin'?" boomed the beast.

"Home," said Mumble.

"Oh yeah, so am I," the Elephant seal replied.

"If you don't mind backing up a little bit, we'll just squeeze past," Mumble said politely.

"That's the one thing I can't do, matey," said the creature. "Bryan the Beachmaster backs up for nobody."

"But we've come all the way across," said Mumble.

"Then you'll just have to go all the way back, won't ya?" replied the Beachmaster.

"But I've got the kids," said Mumble. "It's kind of dangerous."

"Fair enough," said the Beachmaster. "But

see it my way: One day I'll be protecting my beach and some pumped-up punk wants to take it from me. We're nose-to-nose. The whole world's watchin'. And in the back of my mind there's this niggling doubt. I once backed up for a penguin! He'll see it in my eyes and I'm gone. Good-bye, ladies; hello, lonely beach. Ya with me?"

Mumble tried to reason with the Beachmaster, but it didn't work.

"Get out of my way!" roared the Beachmaster, losing his cool.

Bo decided to take action.

"My mother says every obstacle is an opportunity," she said.

In a flash, Bo jumped onto the Beachmaster's nose and backflipped right over him. She was almost on the other side of the bridge, but the Beachmaster flicked his huge tail and sent her flying back, right onto Mumble's chest.

Atticus was not going to stand for this. He waddled up to the Beachmaster and slapped the seal's drooping trunk.

"Yo, dog! You be apologizin' right now or I'm gonna tear you a new nostril!" he said.

"You know he didn't mean that," Mumble said to the Beachmaster.

"That's okay," said the Beachmaster, blowing Atticus backward with one blast of air through his trunk. "I didn't mean *that*, either."

Summoning SvenThink, Erik stepped forward and placed his flippers to his temples. But before Erik knew what had happened, the Beachmaster sucked him up with his trunk like a vacuum cleaner and tossed him backward. Erik landed safely, but he was now on the other side of the crevasse . . . and the Beachmaster stood between him and the other penguins!

Mumble was furious. "You fat mother of all bullies! GET OUT OF MY WAY!"

The Beachmaster reared up and lunged at Mumble, who scrambled back to safety. As he grabbed Bo and Atticus, he watched the enormous seal come crashing down on the ice bridge.

Cruuuuunch! The ice shattered and the Beachmaster dropped into the crevasse.

Mumble was shocked, but also relieved as he looked across to see Erik, safe on the other side. Beside Erik were two baby Elephant

seals—the Beachmaster's pups. They stared into the crevasse, wondering what had happened to their daddy.

Mumble peered over the edge, expecting the worst. But not too far below, the Beachmaster was lying slumped on a ledge.

"Are you okay?" Mumble called down.

"Not exactly," replied the Beachmaster.

The pups were overjoyed to hear their father's voice.

"Daddy! Get back up here!"

"Not sure I can," moaned the Beachmaster.

"There is a way," Mumble said. "But you won't like it."

"You want me to back up, don't ya?" said the Beachmaster.

Mumble knew that if the Beachmaster backed up, he would be able to turn himself around and pull himself up to the top.

"Daddy, we won't think any less of you, promise!" one of the pups said.

"Well, I suppose technically it's just reversing," the Beachmaster said, inching his way along the ledge.

"That's the way," Mumble encouraged him.

As the Beachmaster turned, he lost his footing and teetered on the edge of the ledge. Everyone let out a gasp, but he was able to steady himself.

"Reach out with your trunk! One last *ooomph!*" called Mumble.

Straining and puffing, the Beachmaster curled his snout over the top of the crevasse and grabbed onto the edge. He pulled himself up until he was eye to eye with his pups.

"G'day, boys," said the Beachmaster with a wink just before *crrrraaaak!* The entire ledge supporting the Beachmaster collapsed beneath him and he fell again—but this time much, much deeper down. There was a long silence. Everyone held their breaths until they heard a distant thump. The Beachmaster landed somewhere deep down in the crevasse.

"Daddy? Can you hear us?" cried the fearful pups.

After some time, they heard a faint, shaky voice calling their names. "Shane? Darren?"

Their father was still alive.

"I need you both to be strong," said the dazed Beachmaster. "I know you will 'cause you've never let me down. Penguin? You still there?"

"Right here," said Mumble.

"Would you see that my boys get home safely to their mother?" asked the Beachmaster.

"Daddy?" cried the pups. "What are you saying?"

"Boys, the clock's about to run out on your old man's career."

Tears welled up in the pups' eyes. But Mumble had not given up hope. "Take a good look around down there! Can you see a way out?"

"I'm stuck here," the Beachmaster called back.

"All right, everyone away from the edge, and nobody move till I get back," Mumble said.

"Where are you going?" asked Atticus.

"To see what I can do for their daddy," Mumble replied.

"What can *he* do?" said one of the pups, looking at Mumble. "He's just an ordinary penguin."

The pups turned to Erik, who could only agree with them. His dad certainly couldn't fly down there like Sven could. How could he save an enormous Elephant seal?

Chapter 8

Nearby, Will and Bill finally reached the surface of the ocean and climbed onto a sheet of floating ice.

Will stood to his full height—a whole inch—and declared, "That's one small step for a krill, one giant leap for spineless invertebrates!"

Looking around, Will and Bill realized they were standing on the tail of a dozing Leopard seal. They were staring at the back end of a black hole.

"Holy mother of krill!" cried Bill.

"How's your appetite, Bill? He's a big un!"

Will crouched on the ice and crept farther up onto the Leopard seal's tail.

"What on earth are you doing?" squeaked Bill.

"Shh," whispered Will. "I'm stalking."

"You can't stalk. You're a krill!"

"Less talk, more stalk," snapped Will. "We've got to evolve, Bill."

"Evolve? Just like that? It's taken us millions of years just to get this far!" said Bill as he followed his friend.

"Watch and learn, Billy boy," cautioned Will. "I'm about to naturally select."

Will bit into the seal's blubber, but the Leopard seal didn't notice a thing.

Will thought about the taste. "Mmm, a little chewy. Keenly aromatic with just a hint of . . ."

"Derriere?" Bill offered. "You just nibbled on its butt. Don't let it go to your head."

"*Au contraire!* I shall go to *its* head," exclaimed Will in triumph. "Onward and upward, my friend! Fresh delicacies await!"

Will and Bill began the long climb to the top of the Leopard seal.

Mumble slipped quietly into the water because not far off a huge Leopard seal was dozing on a small ice floe. It happened to be

the very same Leopard seal that the krill were climbing . . . at the very same time.

Mumble swam deep down under the ice shelf until he saw a ray of light illuminating a transparent wall of ice. Through the ice, he could see the Beachmaster slumped motionless at the bottom of a dry cave. There was no time to waste. Mumble hurled himself at the ice wall with his shoulder again and again, trying to break through it and set the Beachmaster free. But it didn't work; the ice was too thick. Mumble had another idea. He headed back to the surface.

Mumble swam close to the ice floe where the large Leopard seal still dozed. Climbing on it, the two little krill had almost reached the summit.

"How far now?" gasped Bill, exhausted.

"The head is just ahead!" cried Will.

Mumble now circled the ice floe, taunting the Leopard seal.

"Hey, dufus! Kelp sucker!" said Mumble, hopping onto the ice.

But the Leopard seal did not stir.

"Oh, I'm sorry," said Mumble. "My mistake. I thought you were a ruthless killing machine."

The seal remained completely still. Mumble

Erik is the tiniest, fluffiest penguin in all of Emperor Land.

**Mumble and Gloria are the center of attention—
the golden stars of Emperor Land.**

**But little Erik doesn't dance—
he just stands still.**

Bo and Atticus, Erik's friends, love to dance and sing.

Erik, Bo, and Atticus run away together to Adelie Land.

Ramon is happily reunited
with his best Adelie penguin friends.

Erik, Bo, and Atticus get to meet
the Amigos in Adelie Land.

In Adelie Land,
Erik meets Sven—
and wishes he could
fly just like him.

In the ocean, best friends Will and Bill
the krill live under the ice.

On the way home to Emperor Land,
the path across an ice bridge is blocked
by a humongous Elephant seal.

To save all the penguins in Emperor Land,
everyone learns to dance together.

Erik realizes you don't need to fly to be
awesome—and that his dad is the greatest!

was as close as he dared to go. At that very moment, Bill and Will were about to reach the top of the seal's head.

"Stand back," Will whispered. "This could get messy."

Will flexed his little thoracopods in preparation for his meal. He bit down hard on the Leopard seal. Just then, the seal opened an eye and lunged at Mumble!

Mumble immediately leaped into the water. The chase was on!

They zoomed through the water, Mumble keeping just ahead of the seal. He twisted and spiraled, leading the Leopard seal toward the wall of ice standing between them and the Beachmaster.

All the while, Will and Bill clung on to the seal's head for dear life.

"He's a fighter," said Will, convinced that the seal's wild twists and turns were all his doing. Of course, the seal didn't know the krill even existed.

"But he'll drop soon!" Will continued. "It's just his death throes!"

As Mumble reached the wall of ice, the Leopard seal moved in for the kill. At the last moment, Mumble darted to one side . . . and the Leopard seal slammed headfirst into the ice wall.

Crrraaaack! As the ice shattered, the astonished Leopard seal found itself on top of the Beachmaster's belly.

"G'day, gorgeous," said the Beachmaster, raising himself up. The Leopard seal took one look at the huge Beachmaster and shot off.

Mumble's plan had worked perfectly. As seawater gushed into the cavern and the crevasse flooded, Mumble and the Beachmaster floated up to the top.

Erik and the pups were delighted.

Back under the ice, Will, too, was thrilled with the success of his first hunting expedition. He and Bill let go of the Leopard seal and watched him swim off in a big hurry.

"Woo-hoo! Did you see the look in his eyes? Mortal terror!" shouted Will in triumph.

Bill was far less enthused. "You said he was finished. Done for!"

"I spared his life, Bill. He'll tell his friends, spread the fear. There's a new predator in town!" yelled Will. "Someone's got to keep the numbers down, Bill. And we are that someone!"

Safely back on the ice, Mumble was reunited with Erik, Atticus, and Bo and the Beachmaster was back with his beloved pups.

"How's that shoulder?" the Beachmaster asked his rescuer.

"It's okay," said Mumble, shrugging it off. But when he shrugged, it really hurt.

"I owe you, my friend," said the grateful Beachmaster. "All you have to do is ask. Any time, any place, anything. No worries. Okay?"

"No worries," said Mumble.

The Beachmaster slid into the water with his adoring pups on his back and swam off toward the horizon.

Mumble turned to the three little penguins gathered around him.

"Kids, I don't know about you, but I can't wait to get home."

As Mumble led the way back to Emperor Land, Erik gave his father a long look before he, too, ambled after them. Maybe his dad couldn't fly like Sven, but he had saved an Elephant seal!

Chapter 9

Later in the day, Atticus and Erik trudged up a long slope while Bo walked along an ice ridge above them. Mumble came to a halt and looked around. It didn't make any sense. Emperor Land should have been right there. Right where they stood!

From her high vantage point, Bo spotted something. "Oh my goodness!" she exclaimed.

Quickly, the others scrambled to higher ground and looked down. The entire Emperor nation was imprisoned by a massive wall of ice—the very wall of ice on which Mumble and the kids were standing. They were on the Doomberg! They realized that the rogue iceberg had slammed into the entrance of Emperor Land, trapping all the penguins below.

"Hey, look! Somebody got out!" came a cry from down in Emperor Land.

Thousands of Emperor penguins looked up hopefully to the top of the Doomberg.

"Hey, buddy, how do we get out?" one penguin yelled.

"I don't know," shouted Mumble. "I'm trying to get in."

The crowd gave a collective groan of disappointment.

"Atticus, my man!" cried Seymour, overjoyed to see his boy again.

"Yo, dad!" yelled Atticus. "What happened?"

"That big old 'berg you're standing on came a thumpin' and a bumpin', and here we are!" Seymour explained.

Gloria pushed her way through the crowd.

"Mumble! Erik! Down here! My beautiful boys! I thought I'd never see you again!"

At the sight of his mother, Erik dashed forward.

"Whoa, Erik!" Mumble shouted. "Back from the edge!"

"Sweetie, you stay real close to your daddy, okay?" Gloria called. "Mumble, what's going on out there?" she asked.

"I don't know. But whatever it is, there's gotta be a way to get you out," Mumble assured her.

"There is a way. We just haven't found it yet," Gloria replied.

"We're searching every nook and cranny for a way out of here," Seymour added.

"In the meantime, Mumble, we've got a lot of hungry kids down here. Can you get us some fish?" Gloria asked.

At the mention of food, hundreds of tearful baby penguins rushed forward, hungrily snapping their beaks.

Mumble knew he couldn't feed that many penguins by himself and racked his brain for a plan.

"There is a way to feed a whole lot of you. I'll go to Adelie Land and bring back some friends. It's going to take some time, so you'll have to be patient. Okay?"

But before Mumble had finished speaking, Bo headed off.

"Where do you think you're going?" called Mumble.

"I'm taking the shortcut!" said Bo.

"No, you're not, you're staying right here," commanded Mumble.

"But I'm very fast."

"I'm faster," said Mumble.

"No, you're not. You're hurt," she said.

"I'll manage," said Mumble, trying to convince himself.

From down below came the voice of Miss Viola. "Boadicea! Do you have a tail feather?"

"Yes, I do!" shouted Bo.

"Then shake it, my dear!" insisted Miss Viola.

Mumble did not like the idea one bit.

Erik wanted to go back to Adelie Land, too, but he knew he could never keep up with the free-running Bo . . . and that Mumble would not let him go!

"Miss Viola, there are all kinds of dangers out there," Mumble warned.

"Not dangers," Miss Viola corrected. "Challenges!"

From his tower, Noah proclaimed, "Now that's the Emperor spirit! Go, lass, and may the wind be at your back!"

And with that, Bo headed off to Adelie Land.

"Find Uncle Ramon. Tell him to bring as

many friends as he can," Mumble called after her.

Miss Viola let out a parting yodel as Bo sped over the rise.

"Yeeodelay-tee-hoo!"

"Yeeodelay-tee-hoo to you, too!" Bo yodeled back, disappearing from view.

Mumble felt a tug on his tail feathers. "Come on, Uncle Mumble. We got some fishing to do," said Atticus, his generous belly growling with hunger. Erik knew they had to start gathering food for the little penguins below.

Diving again and again, Mumble flung fish after fish onto the shore where Atticus and Erik watched them land on a growing pile. Erik grabbed the biggest fish in the pile, and Mumble, Atticus, and Erik all hurried back to Emperor Land with their catch just as the sun was dropping below the horizon.

As he struggled up a steep rise, Erik hauled his huge fish by the tail, barely able to hold it in his tiny beak. Mumble helped him drag it along until, at the top of the slope, Mumble let go of the fish so it could slide down the other side of the hill.

"Okay, you let it go, too," Mumble instructed Erik.

But as the fish slid down the slope toward Emperor Land, Erik jumped onto its back, riding it like a sled! Because the slope was steep, Erik sped faster and faster down toward the edge of the Doomberg.

"Jump off!" cried Mumble from the top of the rise. But it was too late. Erik and the fish ramped into a large bump in the ice. *Woooosh!* Erik and the fish became airborne.

Erik flapped his tiny flippers and squealed. "Up-uppity-up!"

A gust of wind lifted Erik even higher in the air, but a moment later, he fell back onto the ice with a thud. He slid out of control toward the long drop down into Emperor Land.

Desperate to save his son, Mumble threw himself down the hill, landing heavily on his injured shoulder. He just managed to slide ahead of Erik and, with only inches to spare, stopped him from going over the edge.

"Don't ever do that again!" scolded Mumble.

But Erik was not shaken by the close call. In fact, he was delighted.

"I was flying! Really flying!"

"Erik," snapped Mumble, "we are penguins! We can't fly!"

"Sven is a penguin and he can fly!" protested Erik.

Atticus arrived right in the middle of the heated argument.

"I don't know what kind of penguin Sven is," Mumble said. "But we are Emperor penguins—we can't fly and we never will!"

Trying SvenThink, Erik put his flippers to the sides of his head and cried out, "But if everyone could learn to fly, Mommy could get out of there!"

Just then, Mumble and Erik heard a familiar voice from below.

"Hey! What's going on with you two?" asked Gloria, who had heard the disagreement.

"Just working things out," Mumble called out sadly.

Gloria requested a word with her son alone. Mumble sighed and headed off to catch more fish. Atticus stayed with Erik.

"Erik? I want to be right there by your side. But I can't, so I need you to close your eyes," said Gloria reassuringly.

Erik was too upset to really listen to his mother. But then, Gloria began singing a beautiful lullaby. Her exquisite voice floated up and washed over Erik, soothing him. Soon it affected all the penguins around her until they, too, began to hum and sing along with her. And little penguin chicks nearby went into a deep sleep.

Gloria's uplifting song helped all of the Emperors forget their misfortunes and made them feel like a whole nation again.

The stars glowed bright in the night sky, and Mumble sighed as the sweet song reached him on his way back to the sea. On the Doomberg, Erik and Atticus snuggled up and soon fell asleep.

Chapter 10

Mumble was a lonely figure as he trudged across the moonlit ice shelf to get more fish for the trapped penguins.

Deep in the ocean, it was extremely dark . . . except for two lonely krill glowing faintly.

"Will?" whispered Bill. "Are you asleep?"

"Yes," said Will. "Deeply."

"Then wake up and tell me . . . is that a swarm I see before me or am I dreaming?"

Will cast a sleepy eye over a large, glowing shape gently swimming past them.

"You're dreaming," said Will.

Bill was seeing a family of luminous jellyfish floating past—two parents and their many children. There were hundreds of them. Bill thought they looked calm and happy.

"How wonderful," said Bill.

"I wonder if they're edible," said Will.

"Will, don't you long for the patter of a thousand tiny feet?"

"I, for one, don't have the means to bring up so many kids. I mean, the birthday presents alone . . ."

"I've already picked out the names for mine," said Bill. "Phil, Jill, Syl, Gill, Dyl, Hil, Billy, Lilly, Wilma, Willis, Wilbur, Wilhelmina . . ."

Will was getting tired of his sentimental friend's chatter and swam off.

". . . and there is even a Will," said Bill, following him. "You know, Will, we could start a little swarm of our own!"

"We're both males, Bill."

"We could adopt?" Bill offered.

Will stopped and turned to Bill.

"You adopt, I'll adapt. Now if you don't mind, I've got slaughtering to do."

Will was off again.

"Fine. That's fine," said Bill, calling after him. "You go off, then. Quench your bloodlust. There's plenty more krill in the sea!"

Bill looked around. It was dark and he was all alone. He quickly swam back to Will's side.

"You are all the swarm I've got, Will!"

"Suit yourself," said Will. "But no hanky-panky, okay?"

The sun was rising as Mumble headed back to Emperor Land once more, weary from fishing. He limped across the ice with fish spilling out of his beak and more tucked under each flipper. He even kicked a large fish ahead of him with his tired feet.

Just then, a shadow passed over him. Mumble glanced up and saw a fierce-looking Skua bird hovering above him. He knew Skuas were aggressive scavengers—vultures of the ice. This particular Skua was known as Yellaleg.

"Hey, buddy," squawked Yellaleg with contempt. "Ya goin' back n' forth all night. Are you ever gonna give up? Ya half-dead already, so why not go all the way?"

Yellaleg was soon joined by his buddy Brokebeak.

"Yeah, you hit the deck, and we take care of the rest. No mess, no fuss, dat's us!" Brokebeak cackled.

Mumble started walking faster.

As dawn broke over Emperor Land, penguins who had been searching for an escape route reported to Noah the Elder.

"What news have ye?" Noah asked.

Seymour spoke for the search team.

"Noah, we have searched every nook and cranny, but we've found nothing."

"Then look again," Noah urged. "Go back and search a hundred times!"

Another elder penguin, Eggbert, stepped up.

"But, Noah, there's no way out! It's pointless!"

The sky darkened. Noah and the others looked up as thousands of Skua birds swooped down over Emperor Land.

"My all-time favorite," cawed Yellaleg. "Doomed penguin, packed in ice!"

"It's a smorgasbird," chirped Brokebeak.

High on the cliff above, Erik and Atticus were woken by the noise of the attacking Skuas. The two terrified penguins ran for their lives and took shelter in a small, icy crevice. Atticus whimpered softly, and Erik put a protective flipper around him.

A deep unease spread throughout Emperor Land as even more Skuas swept down and circled above the entrapped penguins.

Noah stood tall on his tower of ice, rallying the fearful penguins.

"Stand together! Hold fast! They are scavengers. Cowards! They prey only on the weak, and what weakens us most is fear!"

The Skuas surrounded Noah's tower but he stood his ground.

"Though we stare famine in the face, we will not yield! Though imprisoned on every side by colossal walls of ice, we will not forsake our heritage. As long as this tower stands, so shall we, this glorious Emperor nation!"

There was a moment of silence, and then a large dollop of Skua dropping plopped onto Noah's face. This was the signal for the Skuas to launch a full-scale attack on the colony. Chaos broke out as penguins scattered in every direction. Parents herded their young into caves and crevices as the Skuas snapped at them with their beaks!

Trapped and under fierce attack, would the penguins survive?

Chapter 11

When Mumble arrived back at the Doomberg, he dropped the fish at the terrible sight of Emperor Land under attack below. Not far from him, a gang of Skuas flapped around the small crevice where Atticus and Erik were huddled. Luckily, the kids were just out of range of their sharp beaks.

Enraged, Mumble flopped onto his belly and torpedoed down the slope. He slammed into the Skua pack, sending the birds flying. Then, Mumble saw Gloria down below trying to herd hundreds of frightened baby penguins to safety. Cackling Skuas swooped toward them, beaks snapping.

"Gloria, behind you!" cried Mumble.

Gloria turned just in time to see Yellaleg snatch a stray baby chick in his beak. Gloria raised a flipper and clobbered Yellaleg. The Skua let out a screech and hit the ground hard, freeing the terrified chick.

"Pick on someone your own size, creep." Gloria bristled.

Yellaleg backed away.

"Oh, I will, princess. I'll pick on you first! While you're still fresh. Before you're stiff and stinky," spat out Yellaleg before flying off.

Mumble watched helplessly from above as Gloria, Seymour, and Miss Viola battled with all their strength against the vicious scavengers. But it seemed only a matter of time before the Skua birds would overpower them.

Until . . .

Mumble heard a faint call, a distant but distinctive, "Yodelay-ee-too!"

Miss Viola recognized the sound immediately and responded with her own "Yodelay-ee-too!"

As Mumble turned and Atticus and Erik poked their heads out of the crevice, they saw a little penguin charging over the rise toward them. It was Bo! And she was not alone. Behind her, Ramon and his Amigos led an army of hundreds of Adelie penguins.

"Bo! You did it!" Mumble called. "Ramon! You brought all your friends!"

"You kidding?" said Ramon. "These are just my cousins."

Ramon pointed with his flipper. "Those are my friends."

Mumble could not believe his eyes. More penguins swarmed over the rise, all carrying fresh fish in their beaks. There were penguins of all shapes and sizes: squat little Adelies, blackbacked Magellanics, tiny Fairies, and bearded Chinstraps all carrying fish and marching toward Emperor Land. Leading the group was Lovelace, his colorful vest standing out in the crowd.

Realizing they were greatly outnumbered, the Skuas fled to the skies. Upon seeing their penguin brothers and sisters at the top of the Doomberg high above them, the Emperor nation cheered.

Mumble was humbled.

"Ramon, you're such a true friend. Thank you, amigo."

"Don't look at me," said Ramon. "I had nothing to do with it."

Mumble turned to the other penguin likely to have done this.

"Well then, Lovelace! Thank you!" he said.

"You got the wrong penguin, brother," said Lovelace.

"Then who . . . ?" asked Mumble.

"Hidey-ho there," chirped Sven, hovering into view.

Erik's face lit up at the sight of his hero. "I knew it!" he cried.

"Sven, this is such a wonderful thing you've done," said Mumble.

"Friends, fans, and chums," Sven announced as he settled on top of Mumble's head. "There is much works to be done! We never rest until everybody is fatty! Okay?"

Down at the shore, penguins of all kinds went to work catching fish for the hungry penguins stuck in Emperor Land. They tossed their catch onto the ice, where hundreds more formed a long line and passed the fish from beak to beak all the way back to Emperor Land. Sven flew above the supply line, encouraging them. Then he swooped down into Emperor Land, giving the trapped Emperor penguins a sight they had never seen—a flying penguin!

Soon the first wave of fish arrived, pouring over the edge of the Doomberg into the eager beaks of the waiting penguins below. Sven even flew up to where Noah stood on his tower and dropped a fish into the grateful elder's beak.

Up on the Doomberg, Mumble listened as Atticus, Bo, and Erik told Gloria all about Sven.

"He can carry more fish than any other penguin that ever existed!" Erik exclaimed.

"Ever!" repeated Bo.

"And, it's all due to his uniquely large, red beak!" Atticus added.

"Very impressive," said Gloria.

Mumble signaled to Sven, who fluttered over.

"There's someone down there who's very special," Mumble said, pointing out Gloria.

Sven could not deny her beauty. "Ah, so exquisite."

Mumble nodded and offered a small fish to Sven.

"Knowing Gloria, she won't eat until everyone else has been fed. Do you think you could take this down to her?"

"Mumbley, please! She is your soul mate. She deserves only the very best! Courtesy of me!" Sven insisted as he flew off toward the open sea.

Just below the surface, Will swam along an ice wall, stalking for prey. Bill floated beside him.

Suddenly, a group of penguins appeared before them, catching fish with great enthusiasm.

"A predator convention! Why wasn't I invited?" yelped Will, charging forward.

Bill's heart sank. His friend Will was getting himself into more trouble than he realized. With all eleven legs, Bill grabbed onto Will.

"Get off me!" Will bristled.

"Don't go, Will. You'll never survive!" Bill protested.

Will finally said what had been on his mind for a long time.

"Bill, I think we should split up."

"If it's personal space you want . . . ," said Bill, shifting a little to one side. "How's this?"

"No," said Will. "I mean really split up. This is my life now."

Will was eager to join the pack of feeding penguins. "I'll see you around," said Will, swimming off.

Tears welled up in Bill's eyes.

"Don't leave me, Will!"

Will turned back to Bill. "You'll be fine, Bill. There's nothing to fear," he said.

Just then, a black hole bore down on Will, and he was instantly swept up into the mouth of a fish. This fish was followed by many other fish, all of which were being chased by Sven. Sven scooped up all of the fish into his beak and headed for the surface of the water. And, just like that, Will was gone!

"Please! Somebody? Anybody! I've lost my Will!" Bill whimpered.

But now he was quite alone.

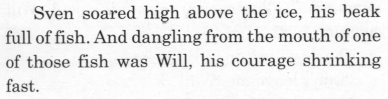

Chapter 12

Sven soared high above the ice, his beak full of fish. And dangling from the mouth of one of those fish was Will, his courage shrinking fast.

Sven hovered above Mumble, and then spiraled down to where Gloria was busy feeding the little chicks.

"Single file, with a smile," she chirped. Sven landed beside her.

"You must be Sven," said Gloria, somewhat startled.

Sven flicked back his golden head feathers.

"Pleased to meet you. I am delightful!" he said through a mouthful of fish. "I bring premium seafood to Glorious!"

Mumble watched from above as Sven moved closer to Gloria, his beak wide open, dripping with fish. Gloria hesitantly leaned in, and Sven unexpectedly lunged forward. There was an awkward moment as their beaks met. This was the perfect moment for Will, still dangling from one of the fish in Sven's beak, to make his escape. Will let out a tiny scream that no one could hear as he jumped. Luckily, he made a soft landing on the head of a baby penguin.

Gloria chose a fish from Sven's beak and swallowed it.

Sven moved closer to Gloria. "If you are not feeling a full Svensation, you can have more."

"Thank you, Sven, but I'm sure there are plenty of others more hungry than me."

Sven swallowed the rest. "See you for supper then?"

"I'm kind of busy," said Gloria.

As Sven fluttered away, Mumble called down, "Honey, are you okay?"

"I'm fine," said Gloria. "Are you sure he's not related to Ramon?"

Mumble and Gloria shared a chuckle. Erik was not amused.

"You shouldn't make fun of someone just because he's different," protested Erik.

"Especially someone who has come all this way to save us."

"You're right, Erik . . ." Mumble began to apologize.

"Yeah, and when Sven teaches everyone to fly, they'll be uppity-up and out of there!" Erik added.

"Erik, that's not going happen," Mumble attempted.

"Wait and see. You just wait and see!" Erik declared as he stormed off with Bo and Atticus.

"Well, it looks like I'll never make the daddy hall of fame."

Meanwhile, down below, the citizens of Emperor Land watched in dismay as the number of fish dropping over the edge slowed and then stopped.

Sven flew off to investigate the holdup in the supply chain.

When Sven reached the shore, he found all the penguins that were fishing now standing on the water's edge, staring out to sea. Something was out there . . . something large and red. Sven instantly recognized it. It was the scientific research ship that he and Lovelace had abandoned in such a hurry. But for some reason, Sven was not happy to encounter the humans again.

Lovelace, on the other hand, was delighted to see them!

"Summon them to the aid of our Emperor brothers!" he told Sven.

To Lovelace's surprise, Sven flew as fast as he could away from the ship.

With Sven gone, all the other penguins were confused about what to do next.

Suddenly Lovelace had a thought: Perhaps the humans could help! But the ship was not stopping; it was passing right by them.

"Sven has gone backward . . . so I can go forward!" Lovelace announced just before he dived into the sea and swam toward a large iceberg nearby.

Onboard the research vessel, something caught the eye of one of the scientists: a small, colorful figure on the peak of an iceberg. Looking through binoculars, the scientist realized that it was their long lost friend Lovelace.

Lovelace thrashed his flippers about wildly and whipped his head back and forth, playing his imaginary guitar.

The scientist ran back inside the ship and returned to the deck with an electric guitar and amplifier. As he played, the sound boomed out across the ocean and Lovelace whirled and twirled his flippers in time to the guitar.

The deck of the ship soon filled with other delighted crew members as Lovelace played his air guitar with great gusto. And when he saw that he had their full attention, he dived into the sea and swam back to shore.

"Follow that penguin!" the scientist called from the deck. Slowly, the ship turned toward the shore. The scientist didn't know exactly where Lovelace was going, but he could tell Lovelace wanted them to follow!

Chapter 13

Meanwhile, Sven landed and huddled behind an ice ledge out of sight of everyone. He breathed fast, trying to fight a sense of rising panic. But he could no longer hold back the distant memory of what happened that day he escaped from the ship. That day he flew up onto the window ledge of the ship's kitchen . . . and witnessed a terrible thing. The chef was roasting a whole row of chickens! This was the moment he realized that these humans fed and fattened up birds . . . to eat them?!

Not far away, all the penguins around Emperor Land heard a loud noise approaching and tilted their heads. *Vwaaarrrooom!* A snowmobile lurched over the rise, with Lovelace perched on the handlebars!

He jumped off the machine as it came to

a halt near Mumble. "Lovelace, this is really great," Mumble said thankfully.

"Mumble, my man, aliens, courtesy of Sven!" he announced as more snowmobiles pulled in behind him.

As the scientists stepped off their vehicles, Erik, Atticus, and Bo edged closer to Mumble.

"It's okay, kids," he said soothingly. "I know they look scary, but they're here to help us."

The scientists made their way to the edge of the Doomberg. They were stunned at the sight of the trapped Emperor penguins below and resolved to help them.

From below, the Emperor nation watched as the rescuers threw bright red ropes over the edge of the iceberg. Some curious baby penguins moved forward to investigate.

On the head of one of these little penguins, Will the tiny krill lay hidden by feathers. He wanted to escape from Emperor Land as much as the penguins. And the giant, red cable dangling before him gave him an idea.

"Where there's a Will, there's a way out!" the krill exclaimed.

He leaped onto the rope, his many legs

frantically climbing upward. Suddenly, the rope began to shake and snow trickled down from above. When Will looked up, he gasped. A gigantic creature was sliding down the rope toward him. Soon there were other humans on other ropes around him, loaded with equipment as they descended into Emperor Land. Will turned around and scrambled back down the rope. Just before the huge scientist was upon him, Will leaped across onto the wall of ice and secured himself in a tiny crack in the ice.

Cruuuunch! Will was almost crushed by a scientist's boot. As the human struggled for a foothold, a piece of ice dislodged—the very piece that Will was grabbing on to. Will plummeted down and fell on the scientist's other boot. He latched onto a bootlace, which took him straight back to the bottom of the rope. But Will's adventure was not quite over.

Crraaaack! A pickax smashed into the ice next to Will, hurling him into the air. He landed on a large, shiny, red device. Spotting a hole in the metallic apparatus, Will scurried down into what looked like a safe, dark place. A thunderous sound quickly made him wonder if this was a wise move.

Haaarrrrraw! Will hadn't realized it, but his safe haven was the inside of a chain saw! A scientist yanked hard on the starter cord. Luckily for Will, the motor didn't start immediately and he was off again, scrambling out of the darkness . . . and straight along the metal blade. Will was feeling light-headed as he dangled from the end of the chain saw.

Another pull and this time the engine revved into action. Desparate now, Will leaped clear and onto the snow below.

Will didn't know it, but the humans were creating a path for the Emperor penguins to escape. The penguins knew it, though!

All the tiny krill could see were gigantic, mechanical obstacles and sharp objects. Will hid under a patch of snow, but soon felt himself rising. He was being lifted in a shovelful of snow.

Thwacko! The snow hit the ice wall . . . and Will with it! With his last ounce of strength, Will clung to the wall by the tips of his thoracopods, straining to pull himself up. Then he heard the blades of the chain saw slicing through the ice. Will had only a moment to jump free. He leaped off the ice wall and flew through the air onto a colorful knitted beanie on one of the rescuer's heads. Trembling in shock, Will buried himself in the warm folds of wool.

♫

The ship's crew made good progress carving out a path to the top of the Doomberg.

Mumble and Erik looked on with a great sense of relief.

"Where will we live when everyone gets out?" asked Erik.

"We'll find somewhere new," said Mumble.

"But what if the same thing happens there?" said Erik.

"We deal with the world one problem at a time," reasoned Mumble. "The important thing is that we'll all be together again."

Just then, a snowflake floated down and settled on Erik's head. Then another and another. The sun disappeared and dark clouds gathered. Soon, the wind began to howl and snow fell thicker and faster. It was a blizzard!

Although the escape path was not finished, it was impossible for the ship's crew to continue working. They quickly packed their equipment, climbed back up the cliff, and jumped onto their snowmobiles. As they sped off, a sudden storm gust whipped a colorful beanie off one of the scientists' heads and blew it down, down, all the way back down into Emperor Land, with little Will still holding on for dear life.

The penguins knew what to do: Huddle, share the warmth, and wait out the storm. All the penguins down in Emperor Land and on top of the Doomberg huddled together.

Mumble drew Erik, Atticus, and Bo to him.

"Stay close, stay warm," he said, but his mind was on Gloria down below, where she had gathered all the chicks into a huddle.

Ramon was perhaps the only penguin enjoying the turn of events. He got to be pressed tightly against Carmen!

"Carmen?" Ramon crooned. "Can't you see? Even nature decrees that we be close together."

Carmen ignored him.

As the blizzard intensified, the penguins huddled tighter, and their heads dropped low to protect themselves from the driving wind and snow. Soon, it was a complete whiteout.

 # Chapter 14

After three days, the sun finally shone again. Emperor Land lay silent, blanketed by a massive dump of fresh snow. And deep under the snow, a fragile little limb emerged. Then, a pair of micro-eyes. It was Will!

The tiny krill blinked. All was calm. He sighed. *Peace at last,* he told himself. Suddenly, the ground began shifting beneath him and Will felt himself moving upward.

He was perched on the beak of a baby penguin as it lifted its head up out of the snow. And this penguin was about to sneeze.

ACHOO! Will was off again, flying through the air, not knowing where he'd end up next.

Sven also emerged from his hiding place and flew above Emperor Land to survey the aftereffects of the storm. The sea had frozen over, and there was no sign of the research vessel—the scientists got to their ship before it became trapped in the ice.

Sven glided over Emperor Land as the penguins began emerging from under the snow.

He had an important announcement.

"Everybuddy! Everybuddy!" he called down. "Winter is coming. The sea, she is very, very far away now. Too much of the ice. I regret to inform, but we cannot, anymore, remain in the catering business."

Upon hearing this news, some of the penguins on the Doomberg started drifting back toward Adelie Land. Seeing this, the penguins stuck down in Emperor Land lost hope.

"You can't leave. Not now," Erik pleaded as Sven flew overhead.

Sven swooped down and landed on the head of a departing penguin.

"Sorry, fluffy one," Sven consoled. "But if we stay, *we* become not alive, too."

While all seemed lost, not everyone had given up. Down in Emperor Land, a penguin hurled himself onto his belly and slid down a slope of fresh snow toward an ice ramp. Hitting it at full speed, he flew high into the air, heading toward the edge of the Doomberg.

All the penguins up top looked over to see what was going on.

The brave penguin didn't have quite enough momentum and fell into the soft snow below. But it inspired another trapped penguin to try. She straddled two penguins on their bellies and sped down the slope.

Erik turned to Sven and pleaded again. "Teach them Sven. Teach them how to fly!"

"Iiii-rik, is not that easy," Sven replied.

All three penguins shot up into the air after hitting the ramp. The crowd of Emperors below cheered as the two booster penguins fell away and the daring one flew toward the ledge, flapping her flippers.

As this was happening, Erik pointed a flipper at those trapped below.

"Help them, Sven. You could teach them all to fly!"

"Not all penguins are created equal," said Sven, avoiding the small penguin's gaze.

"But you're a penguin, and you can fly," Erik insisted.

"I am a little more than a penguin," said Sven awkwardly. "I am a Svenguin. There is a difference, yes?"

At that moment, the ski-jumping female's short flight ended and she, too, fell into the snow at the base of the Doomberg. As soon as she landed, more penguins were headed down the ramp at high speed. The trapped penguins were not going to give up without trying.

And Erik wouldn't let go of his idea. "Tell them what to do, Sven," Erik pleaded.

The crowd around them urged Sven, too. "Do it, Sven. Do it!"

"Well, I guess it's just technique." Sven was talking himself into it as the crowd grew louder. "Go, Sven, go!!"

He swooped down and flew alongside the next group of airborne penguins.

"Okay! Head up! Back straight," he encouraged.

But they, too, fell short and dropped, unhurt, onto the snow below. Behind them, another group of penguins was trying to fly.

"Feel the wind beneath your wings . . .

and up-uppity-up!" Sven instructed them, but they, too, dropped out of the sky.

Then it was Seymour's turn. He was so determined to be reunited with his son Atticus that he had a bigger plan. Perched on top of a pyramid of eleven penguins, he roared, "You're goin' down, gravity!"

The pyramid of penguins sped down the slope toward the ramp and lifted into the air, holding formation. Soon, the lower penguins fell away, leaving Seymour soaring toward his wide-eyed son. "Fly, Dad, fly!" cried Atticus.

Seymour flapped his flippers like crazy. "Atticus, my man! I'm comin'!"

Sven flew underneath Seymour, trying desperately to keep him airborne, yelling encouragement. "Rotate flippers and SvenThink . . . will it, will it, will it!"

For a moment it actually looked like it was going to work, until . . . *waahhuummp!* Seymour hit the ice wall and plummeted to the ground, with Sven still underneath him.

After a few moments, Sven's head popped out from under the pile of snow that Seymour dislodged when he hit the wall. He was groggy and overcome with humiliation and embarrassment. He began sobbing quietly because he knew the game was finally up.

"I is not a Svenguin," admitted Sven. "Not even a penguin."

A murmur ran through the crowd.

Then something amazing happened. Sven bent his back . . . and his spine popped! It sounded like knuckles cracking as his body transformed, changing from a proud, upright, puffed-up Svenguin to a bent-over, humble, little puffin bird.

"I am a puffin," Sven confessed. "Just a little puffin birdie . . . all run out of puff."

The penguins were stunned. The Mighty Sven, not a penguin? Just an itty-bitty bird? No wonder he could fly!

"I'm so sorry, everybuddy," Sven said. "When I lose my homelands, I was very lonely and very afraidy. Then I meet you, and you believe in me, little Sven Tervilliksen from much too far away. It was so nice to have a family again."

And with that, Sven murmured a weak "Uppity-up" and simply walked away.

Chapter 15

Erik was in a state of shock as he watched Sven walk away. He felt sadder than he could ever remember. But another surprise distracted him from any thoughts of Sven.

Out of the corner of his eye he saw a small stream of snow trickle past him and heard a familiar tippity-tip-tap sound. He turned around to see his father dancing! Surely this was no time for dancing, Erik thought.

Mumble tapped his feet harder, and more snow slid down into Emperor Land below. The tip-tapping of Mumble's feet was loosening more and more of the snow! Mumble had figured out a way that might save the trapped penguins below. If enough loose snow could be dislodged, it just might form a snow ramp . . . a path for the Emperors to use to escape.

Soon, Ramon and his Amigos, Lovelace, and the other penguins from Adelie Land caught on to what Mumble was doing. They all began dancing, too. With each stomp, the tempo lifted, and more layers of snow started to shift.

Erik finally understood. His dad had worked out a way to save the Emperor penguin nation! Before long, snow was cascading down into Emperor Land and piling up at the base of the Doomberg.

The Emperors below joined in the dance, adding more good vibes. Even Will the krill—crouched in the snow down in Emperor Land—who had never heard or seen dancing before, couldn't stop his feet from tapping along, too.

But up top, Erik was not dancing.

"Come on, Erik! Every step counts!" Bo encouraged.

Hesitantly at first, Erik tried a little hop-step. Then, slowly finding the beat, he began to dance more and more confidently, until . . . *harooooomph!* One large section of the Doomberg collapsed, with dozens of tap-dancing penguins on it—including Atticus and Bo. The falling penguins tumbled over and over and finally landed in the soft snow down in Emperor Land, startled but not hurt.

Miss Viola was shocked, too, but embraced Bo in a huge hug, overjoyed to hold her daughter again. Seymour wrapped his flippers around Atticus lovingly. But they were soon interrupted by . . . *creeeeeeeak!* They looked up to see more of the Doomberg breaking apart!

Erik felt his feet slipping on the shifting ice and frantically grabbed onto the penguin closest to him, who happened to be Lovelace. With his beak, Erik latched onto a loose thread of Lovelace's knitted vest, which made the wool unravel. Spinning around and around, Lovelace lost his footing as he and Erik slid together toward the edge of the Doomberg!

Seeing what was happening, Mumble launched himself desperately toward the pair. He managed to grab hold of the wool thread between them, and anchor his foot in a crack in the ice.

As Lovelace plunged over the cliff, his vest began unraveling fast, making him spin rapidly toward the ground below. Erik was dragged over the edge a moment after Lovelace and soon both dangled in midair. They were held only by the thin, woolen thread running from Lovelace's vest to Mumble's beak, and then to Erik, whose little beak was firmly clamped on to the end of the thread. Directly below, sharp ice spiked up out of the rubble. Watching from below, Gloria shuddered.

Suddenly Sven arrived to help Erik, flapping as fast as his wings could carry him.

"Erik! I'm coming! Do not be afraidy!" cried Sven. But before he could reach Erik, the thread finally snapped, and there was a midair collision. Sven and Lovelace plummeted to the ground, just missing the jagged ice.

Mumble struggled to hold on to the thread, with Erik still dangling below. Rushing over to help, Ramon and his Amigos took hold of the thread. Together, they were able to pull Erik up and soon he was in the safe embrace of Mumble's flippers.

"It's okay, Erik. From now on we stick together," Mumble reassured his son, who was trembling and holding back tears.

Ramon was relieved that he was able to help rescue Erik, but he was worried about

Carmen. Where was she? Looking down, he spotted her far down in Emperor Land.

He called out to her. "I hate these long-distance relationships."

"Amigos? Do me a favor. I count to three, you push me on two," Ramon explained to his friends. "But don't tell me."

Ramon stood on the edge of the Doomberg, closed his eyes, assumed the dive position, and began the count. One, two . . . and . . . over the edge he went. But his Amigos hadn't done a thing. Ramon had jumped off the Doomberg all by himself!

As Ramon plummeted toward the snow, he yelled, "Carmeeeen! I'm cooooomming!" He hit the snow with a thump, landing right at Carmen's feet.

"I can't believe you did this!" Carmen exclaimed.

"How could I not?" said Ramon.

"But down here, we're doomed," she said.

Ramon put a flipper to his heart.

"A thousand lifetimes up there is nothing to this one exquisite moment by your side. You are my entire world."

Carmen was genuinely moved.

"You're . . . you're beautiful," she said.

"Only on the outside," answered Ramon.

Carmen was in love.

"Ramon, my fallen angel, you chased me until I caught you," she crooned in her silky Latina voice.

The pair linked flippers and stared deeply into each other's eyes.

"Ramon," Carmen whispered. "The earth is moving."

"For you, too?" said Ramon.

"No, it's moving for real!" she squealed.

Another massive tower of ice had broken away from the shifting Doomberg and was jutting out above them.

"Mumble, if that thing falls all the way down . . . ," called a familiar voice from below, "it'll finish the path out of here!" Gloria's voice was full of hope.

That was good enough for Mumble. All the teetering ice tower needed was a nudge, and the trapped penguins had their ramp to freedom. Mumble began tapping his feet and, once more, the penguins around him followed his lead. Erik kept a close eye on his father's moves. Down below, Lovelace rallied the troops.

"My man Mumble needs backup! We've gotta pump up the funk!"

All the Emperors turned up the power of their tippity-tap. Even Will shimmied across the snow and joined the crowd.

As penguins above and below danced, ice and snow fell down behind the leaning tower of ice, tipping it a little farther. But there was not nearly enough snow and ice to make it topple.

Mumble's grand plan wasn't working. Once all the loose snow had fallen, the hard packed snow wouldn't budge. But Mumble was not about to give up. He began pounding out more powerful beats, rallying thousands of penguins to take his cue and stomp on the hard snow.

With his eleven feet, Will tippity-tapped even harder, but he was in danger of being squashed by penguin feet thumping around him. He scampered away and took refuge in a puddle of water.

"It's just not enough," said Mumble up above, growing more desperate.

Sven fluttered above Mumble and settled

on the head of a Chinstrap penguin.

"Attentions, everybuddy! Mumble's foot is hurty!"

"But I have a song and dance from my homelands," Sven offered with a genuine desire to help. "It is in Svenish and goes exactly like this."

Sven began to sing. The tune was cheesy, and his dance wasn't any better. Still, all the penguins gave Sven's routine a chance. What did they have to lose?

Penguins above and below tried to follow his strange dance moves. Mumble watched with hope, but the tower still didn't move.

Mumble turned to Erik. "Come on, son."

"Where are we going?" asked Erik as he followed his father through the crowd.

"To find us a lot more ooomph!" was all Mumble replied.

Behind them, Sven and the others danced with all their might.

But the tower still didn't budge.

Chapter 16

Hiding in his puddle, Will was puzzled by something. The water was beginning to swirl around him, and soon it was dragging him down into the ice. As the ice melted, it drained through a tiny shaft and down into the ice shelf. Will slid down deeper and deeper into this seemingly bottomless ice tunnel.

His heart pounded as the terror ride continued. The tunnel twisted and turned, full of sudden drops, narrow spaces, and enormous caverns. Finally, he found himself treading water in the middle of a dark, watery void. He wasn't dropping anymore, but he couldn't see anything, and he was very frightened.

"Where am I? Who turned out the lights? Is this the end? If only I'd listened to Bill, none of this would have happened," he said. "Oh,

Bill, I'm so sorry . . ."

"That's okay," came the sound of Bill's reassuring voice.

"You were right, Bill, I should have stayed with the swarm."

"No, *you* were right, Will."

Will was amazed just how real this imaginary conversation was starting to feel.

"Oh, great! Now I'm talking to myself. That's the first sign of madness."

"You're not mad, Will," said Bill, slowly becoming luminescent and appearing before his eyes.

"Now I'm seeing things. I'm completely insane!" cried Will, growing hysterical.

Bill slapped his face.

"Ouch!" cried Will. "Bill? Is it really you?"

"There's only one of me in the whole world, Will. You taught me that."

All around them, thousands of tiny krill began to light up.

"Hey! Quiet, you two! We're trying to sleep," came a cry from the swarm.

"Hey, everyone," shouted Bill. "It's Will, he's back!"

On hearing this, millions and then billions of krill lit up, illuminating the dark waters. Will was back in the swarm, home at last! The other krill were delighted to see him. Bill had told them about their adventures, and Will was now famous.

"Wow, it's really him," cried one excited krill.

"All conquering and wise!" shouted another.

"I thought he'd be taller," came a more feeble voice.

"Welcome home, Will," said Bill, happy to have his best friend back by his side.

"But how did you find your way back to the swarm?" asked Will.

"They found *me*," said Bill. "I was on my last five legs."

"I was such a fool," said Will repentantly.

"Will, you're a legend."

"No, those days are gone. The carnivore is over," said Will.

"No, Will, it's because of you that we are all here!" Bill explained. "I told them how the world really works, how there were predators and we had to adapt. I led them here, under the great ice where no one can find us."

"But, Bill, we're still at the bottom of the food chain."

"But we all have a purpose, right, guys?" said Bill to the adoring krill around them.

They all agreed.

"And yours is to change the world," Bill continued.

"But what possible difference could one krill make?" Will asked.

"Wait and see, Will," Bill promised. "You just wait and see . . ."

♪♫

On a crowded beach, Elephant seals were in the middle of mating season. Amid the noise and chaos, two gigantic seals stared each other down. The largest of the pair was Bryan—the Beachmaster—taunting his opponent.

"Wadda you lookin' at?"

"Wadda *you* lookin' at?" the challenger responded.

"Dunno," snarled the Beachmaster. "But it sure is ugly."

The challenger was furious and reared up aggresively.

"Come on, then!"

The Beachmaster reared higher. "*You* come on!"

Just as he was about to body slam his opponent, he heard a voice behind him.

"Excuse me," said Mumble, dwarfed by the pair of Elephant seals. The Beachmaster looked down to see Mumble and tiny Erik stuck close to his father.

"G'day, chief. Wadda you doin' here?" said the Beachmaster amiably.

"I need a favor," Mumble explained.

"For you, champ, anything."

"I need you to come to Emperor Land," Mumble asked. "And bring as many of your kind as possible with you."

"Why?" said the Beachmaster.

"To dance," said Mumble, offering a brief demonstration that drew laughs from the crowd, and particularly the challenger.

"Now why would I want to do that?" replied the Beachmaster.

"To free the penguin nation!" pleaded Mumble.

"I'd love to help ya, sport," said the

Beachmaster. "Maybe after winter or some-thin', okay?"

"That's too late," Mumble insisted.

"Right now I've got problems of my own. The multitudes need me to keep the peace."

"If you don't come now, multitudes will die," Mumble warned.

"You sayin' it's my fault now?" said the Beachmaster, bristling. "Listen, fella, you look after your kind and I'll look after mine."

Mumble was outraged.

"If I thought like that I would have left you in that hole. I saved your life!"

"And I'm gonna save yours?" growled the Beachmaster, losing patience. "Just take your little furball of a son and fluff off or else!"

Mumble was stunned. He turned to Erik.

"Come on, son, we're wasting our time. There's nothing for us here."

The Beachmaster turned back to his challenger.

"Now where was I? Oh yeah, wadda you lookin' at?"

"Wadda *you* lookin at?"

"Dunno . . ."

Erik watched as his father limped away. It seemed that all was lost. But Erik refused to give up.

He directed his heartfelt words at his departing father.

"No, Pa, this is so unfair, after all you have done. Nothing makes sense in this world. It's all a big pile of crazy . . . and the kings are all fools!"

Mumble turned around, surprised. He could hardly believe his ears. Erik had never done or said anything like this before!

Once he had his father's attention, Erik turned and glared fiercely at the Beachmaster.

"Where is the honor, when a solemn promise is just a pretty lie—and the mighty mock the courage of the humble?"

The huge Elephant seal also could not believe that these poetic words were coming from such a tiny penguin.

The Beachmaster's pups were transfixed by Erik. This kid was *really* cool.

The passion and feeling rose in Erik's strong, clear voice.

"Although he is just an ordinary penguin,

my daddy taught me, you don't need to be colossal to have a great heart. You don't need to fly to be *awesome* . . . like my hero, my father."

Erik ran over to his father and buried his face in his feathers. All of the Elephant seals fell silent. Mumble was speechless, too. He wrapped his flippers around Erik, still wondering how these extraordinary thoughts and words could have emerged from his beloved, little boy. Had a father ever been so praised by a son? And had a father ever been so proud of his son?

The Beachmaster's pups looked up at their own father, their large, round eyes showing their shame and expectation.

Chapter 17

Back in Emperor Land, Sven was a lone figure at the top of the Doomberg. In utter frustration, he was trying to shift the leaning tower of ice by repeatedly throwing his body against it. But he was making no impact.

Suddenly, he heard something that sounded like rolling thunder. Sven stopped to listen and flew into the sky to investigate. From there he saw it: thousands of huge Elephant seals coming over the rise heading to Emperor Land.

Following them were the penguins who had given up hope of rescuing the Emperors and had been on their way back to Adelie Land!

Down below, Gloria, Seymour, Atticus, Miss Viola, Bo, Lovelace, Ramon, and Carmen heard the strange roaring noise, too. Soon all the Emperor penguins saw what, under normal circumstances, would have terrified them. Leading the giant seals was the Beachmaster with his pups by his side . . . and on his back was Erik, wrapped tightly in Mumble's flippers.

"At the edge of disaster, here comes the Beachmaster!" Lovelace called as they arrived.

All the trapped penguins waited with great anticipation, not sure what would happen next.

Bryan the Beachmaster stopped at the edge of the Doomberg and surveyed the problem. The Doomberg seemed much too big to shift, even with the massive bulk of the Elephant seals.

"Gee, matey, now I realize what you want us to do. This could be too much, even for all us big fellas put together," Bryan confessed.

Huge seals around him nodded their agreement. Some were already growing restless and impatient. Mumble worried that they would give up and leave without even trying. The Elephant seals were his last hope to free the trapped penguins.

Mumble didn't know what to do next. But Erik did.

"Dad, show them happy feet," Erik urged.

Mumble smiled at Erik and began his

famous tip-tap-tippity-tapping, this time adding some *stomp*. Erik picked up his father's beat and danced along to the rhythm. The Beachmaster's pups joined the chorus.

The tip-top-tapping and the skit-scat-scatting soon infected the Beachmaster, who began shaking his large body. The other Elephant seals began to follow, flapping their large tail fins and flipping their flippers. As the gargantuan creatures threw themselves around, some of the snow began to fall over the edge, packing in behind the tower of ice.

Everyone was singing and dancing in time to the new happy-feet beat. *Tip-tap-tippity-stomp!* Mumble announced it was time to kick it up a notch, and the Beachmaster responded instantly. In time to each beat, he slammed his huge belly hard onto the tightly packed snow. Thousands of Elephant seals did the same. Large pieces of snow and ice began to shift as the great weight of the Elephant seals broke up the deep layers of the Doomberg.

Beneath the Doomberg, Will and Bill heard

the rhythms coming from above them.

"You hear that?" said Bill.

"They're doing it again," said Will.

"Doing what?"

"This," said Will as he began dancing upside down on the ice, his little legs tapping out a neat series of rhythms.

"Try it!"

Bill did his best to mirror Will's dance moves.

"Fascinating," he said.

The pair danced in tandem, tippity-tapping with all twenty-two legs.

"What do you call it?" said Bill.

"I have no idea," said Will.

All around them, billions of their fellow krill joined in, tippity-tapping underwater against the ice.

"But what is it for?" asked Bill.

Will couldn't quite explain it.

"It just brings out my . . . happy!"

That was a good enough reason for the entire swarm to dance harder and faster under the ice.

Chapter 18

High above the billion dancing krill, penguins and Elephant seals danced and stomped. The Beachmaster backed up and then bounded forward onto the hard-packed ice.

Thuuddddudadud!

"Sometimes you've got to *back up* to go forward!" declared the Beachmaster.

The other Elephant seals got the hang of it, and soon they were all backing up and slamming their bodies onto the ice. Large chunks of ice and snow flooded down behind the leaning tower of ice. It began to tip a little more, looking like it would topple.

The trapped penguins were uplifted. Lovelace swung his air guitar in time to the rhythm, and Bo backflipped across the snow. At the top of the massive iceberg, every variety of penguin—

Adelies, Chinstraps, Fairies, and Megallanics—danced in time with the Elephant seals.

Among all this excitement, one lonely creature wasn't dancing. But this time it wasn't Erik—it was Sven.

"Hey! Come on!" Mumble called to him.

Sven pointed a flipper at himself. "Who, me?"

"Every step counts!" said Erik.

Sven's eyes lit up as he began to dance alongside Erik.

Mumble, swollen with pride, called to his mate. "Gloria! Check this out!"

Gloria could not believe it. She had never seen Erik so involved and happy before. She sang out in time with Erik's dancing.

Under the combined power and weight of the penguins and seals, the entire Doomberg began to shake. Slabs of snow and ice streamed over the edge behind the leaning tower of ice until . . .

It finally began to creak and shudder.

As the ice shook above, the swarm of dancing krill beneath the ice resembled a light show. In the center, Will broke into a solo, his legs tip-tapping complex rhythms.

Will spun around in a circle and lifted one